Waltzing Matilda

Scholastic Press
345 Pacific Highway
Lindfield NSW 2070
An imprint of Scholastic Australia Pty Limited (ABN 11 000 614 577)
PO Box 579
Gosford NSW 2250
www.scholastic.com.au

Part of the Scholastic Group
Sydney • Auckland • New York • Toronto • London • Mexico City
• New Delhi • Hong Kong • Buenos Aires • Puerto Rico

First published by Scholastic Australia in 2006.
This edition published in 2017.
Illustrations copyright © Freya Blackwood, 2006.

National Library of Australia Cataloguing-in-Publication entry:
    Paterson, A. B. (Andrew Barton), 1864-1941.
    Walzing matilda.
    ISBN 9330303003158
    I. Blackwood, Freya. II. Title.
A821.2

Typeset in Adobe Jenson.

Printed in China by RR Donnelley.

10 9 8 7 6 5 4 3 2   17 18 19 20 21 / 1

In Gratitude.

A WONDERFUL MOTHER.

Thanks to Kate Blackwood for assistance in
research, for encouragement and provider of
unending support. FB

Waltzing Matilda

AB PATERSON   FREYA BLACKWOOD

A Scholastic Press book from Scholastic Australia

Cold rain continues from the south, but
like a dirty night.

Richmond
Hughenden
McKinlay
Kynuna
Combo
Waterhole
Dagworth
Ayshire
Downs
Middleton
Winton
U E E N S L
Longreach
Barcaldine

Once a jolly swagman camped by a billabong,

All shearers at Dagworth station have refused to sign the pastoralists' agreement, and are now on their way to Winton. It is expected that non-union shearers will be brought in to shear the 120,000

BUSHRANGER ON RAMPAGE

CLONCURRY, SATURDAY.

The infamous bushranger Black Bearded Tom escaped police clutches yesterday after raiding a coach travelling from Cloncurry to Brisbane. The coach was stopped just outside the settlement of McKinley at o'clock. Black Bearded Tom held ers, Mr. and Mrs. Butler, their ughter and coachman captive while removing ne aluables from the coach. He then f seback towards Kynuna.

Black Bearded Tom is wanted b

ce of a reed robbery. Any i

whereabouts should

risbane polic

Under the shade of a coolibah tree;
And he sang as he watched and waited till his billy boiled
'You'll come a-Waltzing Matilda with me.'

A-Waltzing Matilda, Matilda my darling,
You'll come a-Waltzing Matilda with me;
And he sang as he watched and waited till his billy boiled—
'You'll come a-Waltzing Matilda with me.'

REFUSAL TO SIGN THE AGREEMENT

[By Electric Telegraph.]

(FROM OUR OWN CORRESPONDENT)

THARGOMINDAH, August 2

The shearers have refused by either
Margaret, and a camp has been
100 m

REFUSAL TO SIGN AGREEMENT.

[BY ELECTRIC TELEGRAPH.]

Public Notice

THE SHEARERS' UNION QUEENSLAND.

SUPPORT the SHEARERS' STRIKE!

DON'T let the SCABS take your job and your livelihood. JOIN the Union camps at Coombemartin, Winton or Hughenden.

HOLD out for 30s per 100 and the terms of the SHEARERS' UNION. JOIN the Union camp at Fifteen-mile Bend Creek, 4 miles from HUGHENDEN.

Down came a jumbuck to drink at the billabong;

Up got the swaggie and grabbed him with glee;

And he sang as he stowed that jumbuck in his tuckerbag—
'You'll come a-Waltzing Matilda with me.'

ESDAY, JULY 31, 1894

THE SHEARING DISPUTE.

ARRIVAL OF NON-UNIONISTS.

POLICE ESCORT FOR PROTECTION.

THE SHEARING DISPUTE.

ENGAGEMENT OF NON-UNIONISTS.

CONTINGENT FROM THE SOUTH.

[BY ELECTRIC TELEGRAPH.]

(FROM OUR OWN CORRESPONDENT.)

ROCKHAMPTON, July 26

The steamer Eurimbla, which left Melbourne on Tuesday for Rockhampton, had on board forty shearers under engagement to the Central Queensland Pastoralists' Association. These will be thirty-five in Brisbane by a large number engaged other men require will arrive here next week. In previously engaged further contingent will join them. shed at their own exp been promised extended contingent will arrive for othe.

The
Pastoral at
place of
o'clock

Immediately on their arri

Bowen Down THE SOUTH.

WANING SUPPLY OF FREE LABOUR.

ARRIVALS FROM NEW ZEALAND.

[BY ELECTRIC TELEGRAPH] twenty rouse

ating that

A-Waltzing Matilda, Matilda my darling,
You'll come a-Waltzing Matilda with me;
And he sang as he stowed that jumbuck in his tuckerbag—
'You'll come a-Waltzing Matilda with me.'

Down came the squatter mounted on his thoroughbred;

A BRAVE POLICEMAN. Down came policemen one, two, and three.
... in the jumbuck tr...

Up came the troopers—one, two, three.

'Who's the jolly jumbuck you've got in your tuckerbag?
You'll come a-Waltzing Matilda with me.'

A-Waltzing Matilda, Matilda my darling,
You'll come a-Waltzing Matilda with me;
'Who's the jolly jumbuck you've got in your tuckerbag?
You'll come a-Waltzing Matilda with me.'

Up got the swaggie and jumped into the billabong.
'You'll never catch me alive,' said he.

And his ghost may be heard as you pass by that billabong—
'You'll come a-Waltzing Matilda with me.'

A-Waltzing Matilda, Matilda my darling,
You'll come a-Waltzing Matilda with me;
And his ghost may be heard as you pass by that billabong—
'You'll come a-Waltzing Matilda with me.'

A Short History of a Long Tradition

◆

'Waltzing Matilda' is said to have been composed to fit a tune that Banjo Paterson heard a young woman playing in January 1895. The young woman was Christina Macpherson, whose father was a rich squatter who owned the *Dagworth* station in northern Queensland.

Just before Paterson visited, there had been a number of big strikes in the area. These strikes were led by sheep shearers. The shearers wanted better pay, but the station owners (who were mostly rich squatters) didn't want to give it to them. So the shearers refused to work until they were offered more money. There was a lot of violence and suffering. The shearers' families went hungry, and fights broke out when other workers (known as 'scabs') were brought in to do the shearing.

One story claims that a shearing shed at *Dagworth* was burnt to the ground by angry strikers, and that the violence got so bad that shots were fired. This story says that the strike leader was found dead beside a billabong the next day.

Paterson is said to have written this song in honour of the shearers and their leader. Freya Blackwood's illustrations follow this tradition.

'Waltzing Matilda' was first published as a song in 1903. This version was slightly different, both in tune and words, to the one that Paterson had written earlier. However, it is the one that became better known. The version of 'Waltzing Matilda' that Freya Blackwood has chosen is the original that Paterson wrote in 1895.

'Waltzing Matilda' is regarded as Australia's unofficial national anthem.

Glossary

◆

billabong: a waterhole that only fills up duri rainy season.

billy: a tin container with a wire handle for bo water and making tea.

coolibah tree: a type of eucalypt that grows in pla that are regularly flooded.

jumbuck: another word for a sheep.

matilda: a swag, or a bedroll that is carried like a backpack. Matilda is also a slang word for something that has been stolen.

squatter: in the past, those who settled on land without permission were called squatters; they usually chose the best land available and became very wealthy.

swagman: a man who travels around the countryside with his swag, and who survived by doing odd jobs for farmers, or by begging.

tucker: food.

tuckerbag: a bag used for carrying food.

waltzing matilda: this can mean either carrying your swag about the countryside, or carrying away a stolen item (in the case of this song, a sheep).